HIS
DOGGED
DEVOTION

Copyright © 2024 Mari Mendoza

His Dogged Devotion

All rights reserved. No part of this publication may be used or reproduced in any form or by any means, without written permission from the author, except for brief quotations in reviews. This is a work of fiction.

Names, characters, places and incidents either are products of the author's imagination or are used fictitiously. Any resemblance to actual persons, living or dead, or actual events is purely coincidental.

Table of Contents

CHAPTER I 7
CHAPTER II 21
CHAPTER III 35
CHAPTER IV 43
CHAPTER V 49
CHAPTER VI 53
CHAPTER VII 79
CHAPTER VIII 89
CHAPTER IX 93
CHAPTER X 101
Epilogue 107
Other Books 111

CHAPTER I

Lauren

Lauren Montes lived for her afternoon walks. As much as she loved working from her studio apartment, after working for eight hours, she started feeling the onset of cabin fever. Her mind would convince her that her medium-sized apartment was a shoebox... as if she didn't willingly set up her life here.

She stretched her arms above her head and twisted her body, feeling her bones crack and muscles relax. Lauren had been sitting in front of her desk all day, working on a proposal for a new project. She was creating a bid to land a gig she really wanted. It was a five illustration contract for a well known cosmetics company's new product campaign. She was knee-deep in researching 17th-century England because of it. If she got the job, she planned to celebrate by re-watching Bridgerton. But for now, it was time for a break.

Luckily, there was a park nearby, and she had promised herself and her rescue dog, her adopted daughter, Bonnie, that they would go out for their daily walk.

"Bonnie, come!" It was like she'd pushed a button. Immediately, she heard the sound of dog claws clambering over her tiled floors. Her six-year-old pit bull entered her office after clumsily gliding in front of her door. Bonnie plopped down in front of her, tail spinning helicopter-style, drawing a laugh from Lauren. "You trying to fly away with that tail?"

Tongue lolling to the side of her mouth, Bonnie bobbed her head. Was she nodding?

Lauren couldn't help herself. She went down to rub her baby's sides. "Are you ready? Are you?" Baby talk was inevitable when her face was this close to Bonnie's. The tail wag became more boisterous after she said the magic word. "Ready for our *walk*?"

Pitbulls only had a bad rep because some bad people decided to use them in dog fights. But the moment Bonnie smiled at Lauren in the dog shelter five years ago, she'd fallen head over heels in love. Who wouldn't have? Bonnie had chocolate brown fur, a white chest, and the goofiest smile to ever exist on a face that simultaneously sported fangs.

Lauren stood up to grab her coat and Bonnie's leash. Bonnie dropped down on her front legs, begging for her to hurry up.

"Sit!" She smiled as Bonnie promptly dropped her butt on the floor. Her tail hadn't stopped its helicopter motion even as Lauren guided her paws through the harness. It was like her tail couldn't contain her excitement. "Wait! Let me put on my shoes first." Bonnie understood the command and waited. She knew they were minutes from leaving.

Lauren fastened the buckle on Bonnie and cooed, "Good girl."

They walked out of their apartment into the cool, brisk air. With Bonnie's usual antics, Laren was already in a much better mood.

Today's winter air wasn't too cold. It wasn't her favorite season, but this was a good kind of cold. Plus, winter sunsets were *pretty.* The sun hung low in the sky, casting a warm, golden glow over the park as Lauren strolled along the winding path, her Bonnie happily trotting beside her. She looked back to the skyline. Skyscrapers stood like towering pillars in the background, their glass facades reflecting the sunlight. She took out her phone to take a few pictures. She probably had a hundred of these stored on her phone, but she didn't care. Each sunset felt like a healing experience.

Lauren was stupidly walking backward, distracted by one of the most magnificent sunsets she'd seen this year when she bumped into a firm chest. The collision was gentle but Lauren jumped and fell forward. The stranger reached out to keep her from falling on her face. She winced, cheeks flushing with embarrassment.

She twisted around to apologize only to come face to chest—a very wide very male chest dressed that was stretching a white dress shirt—with a stranger. Her eyes drifted upwards and all thoughts flew out of her head when she locked eyes with a disturbingly attractive hulk of a man.

She had to crane her neck and step back. In the process, she almost stumbled again. The man tightened her grip on her arms. As cliché as it was, time seemed to slow as a spark traveled between them through the contact. Or at least, that was how it felt for Lauren. It must be those historical romance novels she'd been eating up as part of her 'research'.

"Sorry..." she mumbled, blinking way too fast as she tried to regain her composure.

"It was my fault," he said in a deep smooth voice. Her heart fluttered in her chest. She felt lightheaded and floaty? Like she was swimming in that decadent cafe latte she drank this morning. "I should have stepped aside. Are you okay?"

She felt self-conscious. The man was dressed to the nines. Who walked their dog in a dress shirt and slacks? She was freezing her ass off in her coat. She didn't even brush her hair.

"Yes." She swallowed. "I shouldn't have been walking backwards like that. It's just that watching the sunset against the skyscrapers' windows is my favorite part of the day and I was way too excited that I just started shooting without thinking and apparently I hadn't stopped walking," she rambled with a nervous laugh.

Bonnie sniffed the stranger's dog. She tugged the leash, but Bonnie didn't listen to her. "I'm sorry

"Looks like our furry friends want to meet each other as well," he said, gesturing to the dogs now engaged in a friendly sniffing session.

As well? Did that mean he wanted to meet her too? *There's no way.* She quickly chided herself. Becoming a social pariah had made her delusional. Warmth spread through her. "Seems like it. I'm Lauren, by the way."

"Zaid Cervantes," he replied, extending a hand. Lauren braced for the inevitable 'sparks' that seemed to follow any physical contact from him. She still felt like she'd been electrocuted, but at least she was better prepared.

Meanwhile, their dogs continued to sniff and circle each other. Both held their tails high in the air, each deliberate wag slicing through the wind as they worked through the curious but cautious stage of their relationship. They were seconds away from becoming lifelong friends. Lauren could feel it.

As expected, in what seemed like a split second later, Bonnie jumped and they stopped circling each other. She then went still with only her tail moving around, swiping small circles. When Zaid's dog barked in response, Bonnie replied with full-body excitement. Zaid's dog raised his butt, nose angled in a way that made it clear he was preparing to stalk his way closer to Bonnie.

"Clyde. Heel." Zaid's dog stopped what he was doing, which was sniffing Bonnie's butt, and sat down beside his owner.

"Wow," Lauren breathed. Bonnie was obedient, but Zaid's dog had a police dog level of discipline. "His eyes are beautiful."

"He's a husky pitbull mix." His giant dog let out a single bark, chest puffing out in what seemed like pride. Bonnie dropped down and flipped over, baring her white belly.

"Bonnie," Lauren hissed, embarrassed. If this was doggy flirting, Bonnie was an inch from giving everything away on the first few minutes of their first date.

Zaid's pitsky sniffed, tail swaying side to side. "Clyde, behave," Zaid said with a bemused smile as they watched his dog visibly exercise restraint. Bonnie was still on her back, legs opened wide. Lauren could kind of understand. "Her name's Bonnie?"

Lauren had enough self-awareness to reply, "Yes, as in Bonnie and Clyde. But, well, I don't know. She'd had that name when I adopted her."

"Huh. Interesting." The corner of his mouth tipped up to form a grin. It completely transformed his face, making him look younger, giving him a roguish—Lauren gulped. She was losing it, using words like roguish for a stranger. If she continued this line of thought, she was going to end up calling him a rake or something. "I think my dog is in love with your dog. Rest assured, he's the best damn dog on the planet."

Lauren giggled. What could be cuter than this tall man acting like his dog's wingman. She looked up to find him staring at her quite intensely. "You named him after Clyde as in–?"

"Bonnie and Clyde? No, my great-grandfather had a dog named Clyde. He'd just passed away when I got this one." He watched their dogs sniff each other's butts. "But from the looks of it, their names fit them well."

Lauren agreed. "What do you know… Bonnie and Clyde together in Vatan Valley Park."

"Yes. Feels like fate." His eyes were twinkling as he shifted his gaze to study her. She felt his warm gaze roam from the top of her head down to her toes and back up again. Holy hotness. The air between them crackled with an electric charge. She found herself gravitating toward him. The world around them blurred. It felt like they were the only two people in the park. Lauren felt a connection forming between them. It felt like a promise of something scary and unpredictable.

"I hope you don't find me too forward, but I have to say You're the most beautiful girl I've ever had the pleasure to lay eyes on."

She was dumfounded, still reeling from his effect on her. "You're… just being nice?"

Zaid huffed a laugh. "I'm not nice, little rabbit. And the things I'm thinking about in relation to you aren't *nice*."

'Little rabbit' and 'nice' had never sounded dirtier. Vivid images of them together assaulted her. She was being swept off her feet by a cascade of overwhelming… feelings. Until he suddenly asked, "Do you know that man in the black hooded jacket?"

Lauren looked over to the side and spotted a figure lurking next to a tree. A cold chill ran down her spine. "He's here," she whispered.

"Who is 'he' exactly'?"

"Gerald. He's… uhh…" How weird would it be if she said Gerald was obsessed with her? Would Zaid even believe her? The police certainly didn't. She wasn't a celebrity. She wasn't even very pretty. She could kind of understand why they felt like she didn't 'deserve' a stalker. It was the truth though, and apparently she wasn't capable of saying anything but the truth when Zaid was staring at her like this. "He's been, uhh, following me."

Zaid's face immediately clouded over. His stance changed, and If he looked intimidating before, now he looked downright dangerous. "He bothering you?"

"Not really? I mean…" She remembered the things the police said. That he was just admiring her. That there was nothing they could do. That maybe she should just be flattered for the attention.

The all-too-familiar anxiety bubbled at the pit of Lauren's stomach. A complete 180 from what she'd felt a while ago when she'd met Zaid. This afternoon just went from a romantic meet-cute to a potential thriller catalyst and she wasn't happy about it.

Bonnie went on alert. Her ears perked up.

Lauren seized up. She subtly folded over herself, trying to make herself smaller and less visible. She should've worn her coat with a higher collar. She should've worn dark glasses and a cap. Never mind that it was getting dark out. The less attention she attracted, the better her chances were of losing her stalker.

She was too preoccupied with her own thoughts that she barely registered Zaid walking over to the tree beside her.

He was marching to her stalker. Lauren watched as they exchanged a few words. Zaid stepped close to Gerald and socked him in the gut. Her stalker doubled over. Zaid held him by the shoulder, supporting him as if they were friends and he was just drunk. Zaid was smiling, but his eyes were cold. Whatever he was saying was making Gerald paler with each word. Gerald glared at Lauren before nodding and finally Zaid released him. Gerald was limping.

A few passersby glanced at Zaid, only to quickly avert their gaze. Some whispered to each other. Some abruptly changed direction. Everyone gave him a wide berth.

Lauren suddenly realized how others saw him. He looked in control and exuded confidence. Intimidating was too small a word for him. But more than that. He looked like he had little care for how others saw him. With the scar on his face and the set of his jaw, with the tattoos on his knuckles, he looked like he had little care even for the law.

"What did you do?" she asked when he was back in hearing distance.

"I made it clear that his presence was unwanted and if he insists on staying, he will be forcibly removed if necessary."

"I… thank you." Everything was happening so quickly. Her heart was still trying to dispel the extra adrenaline coursing through her body.

"Don't thank me yet, little rabbit."

Little rabbit? She was too overwhelmed to focus on the ridiculous nickname. "Why shouldn't I thank you?"

"Because I'm objectively not any better than him, and I plan to erase your memories of him with mine." He smirked. "I promise to make sure mine are… pleasurable."

She didn't know what to say to that. Why was that hot?

"Would you like to have dinner with me? Or would you rather I walk you home?" He leaned closer to her, making his next words more intimate. "Please give me one date."

She let out a weak laugh, thinking he was joking. He stared at her as if he was waiting for an answer. Oh, he wasn't joking! Why in the name of all things holy did he want to go out with her?

"You want a date? With me?"

He smiled at her, charm dripping from his pores. "I'm desperate for a date, little rabbit."

"Date. Okay."

"Perfect." He offered her his arm and led her to his car.

She'd sounded stupid, but somehow, she'd set a date with the hottest man she had ever laid eyes on. That was a definite win, right?

CHAPTER II

Lauren

"I don't think I'm dressed for this place." Lauren almost turned around and went back to his car. It didn't matter that she'd realized she could end up in a ditch somewhere once she'd sat in it earlier. The threat of being judged for being underdressed was enough to make her want to go back in.

"Don't be ridiculous." Zaid gripped her arm tighter to keep her from bolting. "I'm the one who should be sorry. You deserve a better first date than this."

"What are you talking about? I would've been over the moon with The Heirs. *This* is the most sought after restaurant in Vatan Valley. I thought only famous people ate here!"

"Hmm... I think I'm going to enjoy spoiling you until I've convinced you otherwise. I want you to expect bigger things from me."

Her mind went straight to the gutter. Based from his little smirk, he knew what he said. And he knew she knew what he was trying to say. Lauren zipped her mouth close, unwilling to make a fool of herself by attempting a witty reply. They followed the hostess who led them to the back of the restaurant to a private room. He pulled out her chair for her. "I really should apologize. I would have closed down the place for you. But given the short notice, the only reasonable option was this."

"How did you even get us a seat? I heard that you have to make reservations months in advance."

"I have my ways."

Lauren fidgeted with the edge of her napkin as Zaid slid into the seat across from her. She wondered how many strings Zaid had to pull to get a table. She was also starting to suspect what Zaid did for a living.

"Do you like it here?"

She knew this place charged an arm and a leg for a small plate of pasta. She never understood the appeal. She looked around. The place was small and dark—sorry, *cozy*—which meant it was intimate and nerve-wracking. "Sure."

The corner of Zaid's eyes crinkled as he smiled. Why did she find that so attractive? "We can leave if you want."

"No!" She would never! She hated causing inconvenience to anyone.

He stared at her for a fraction of a second longer than appropriate. He sighed. "Little rabbit. I'm your servant."

She felt like she'd swallowed her tongue.

"I'm saying, I'll do anything you want. Just tell me and I'll make it happen."

Dirty thoughts raced through her mind. Trying to ignore the pulsing between her legs, she just nodded.

"So. Tell me the truth. Where do you want to eat?"

"Here is fine." She smiled. "Really."

Zaid nodded. "Want to tell me about that guy in the park?"

"That was nothing. What were you doing in the park?" she deflected. She was so used to redirecting attention from herself and her problems. It was easier and more comfortable for everyone involved.

"I was doing some surveillance for work."

"Surveillance?"

"My boss has lots of dangerous enemies."

"Don't tell me you work for the president..." she joked.

His eyes flashed. "Not quite."

A chill ran down her spine. "You don't work for the mafia, do you?"

He smiled while keeping an impressively neutral expression. "Your turn, rabbit. Who was that man?"

"Oh." He hadn't let that go. That made her melt a little bit inside. She wrung her hands on her lap. "It's not a nice story."

A shadow crossed over his face. He leaned forward and put a finger under her chin, forcing her to look at him. "I want to know."

That just about broke her. She took a deep calming breath and tried to sound nonchalant. "He'd been following me for a year now. He hasn't really done anything."

"Except scare you shitless," he growled angrily. "You don't have to worry about him now."

Tears pricked her eyes. The police had brushed away her concerns. "Thank you."

"Fuck it. I didn't mean to make you cry." He visibly shook himself. "I apologize. This isn't an appropriate topic for the dinner table." His face broke into a smile. "Why don't you tell me something interesting about yourself?"

At the sudden topic change, she just blurted out the first thing that came into her mind. "I like to relax by reading historical romance." She must have lost her mind. Oh well, he probably had no idea what 'historical romance' encompassed.

"Smutty ones?"

She gasped. "Oh god, how do you know?"

"My mother had a lot of them laying around the house. I might borrowed one or two while growing up." He grinned at her. "What's your favorite novel? Maybe I've read it."

She wasn't sure if she was aroused or embarrassed. "How to Seduce a Rake by Lyra Smith."

"Huh. Not sure if I've read that one. Where and how did the main characters have sex? That might jolt my memory."

She bit her lower lip. A smile crept up her face. "The first scene was in a garden during a party."

"Ah. One of the best places to have a scene."

She chuckled. "Enough about me! Any other guilty pleasures or quirky hobbies?"

His eyes danced as he replied, "I'm actually a closet chef. I love experimenting with new recipes. Last week, I attempted a three-course meal inspired by flavors from different countries. Let's just say my kitchen looked like a delicious disaster zone."

"That's… surprisingly normal."

Zaid's eyes gleamed with amusement. "What were you expecting little rabbit?"

"I dunno. Something like rabbit hunting," she muttered under her breath. He seemed to have super sonic hearing and heard her anyway.

"Ah. It's our first date. I didn't want to scare you."

"I'm tougher than I look." She puffed out her chest. His eyes strayed down to her breasts.

"I don't doubt that for a minute, but it wouldn't be polite to tell you how I'd been imagining what color your nipples are. My mouth is salivating over the thought of feasting on you. Make no mistake, I'm quietly but meticulously planning how I'm going to have messy lovely sex with you."

The server walked in with a smile and stood next to Lauren. "Are you ready to order?"

Zaid snarled at the waiter. "I already put in an advance order." The server froze in place. Zaid and the server stared at each other for a microsecond. Zaid snapped his teeth and the waiter scrambled away.

Lauren bit back a smile. She shouldn't encourage this behavior. "Calm down. He was just doing his job."

"What do you mean? He was standing too close. I'm the only one who can stand that close to you."

He was a little crazy. But she might be crazier... because here she was thinking that a girl could get used to his brand of crazy. She squirmed in her seat.

"I booked a private room for a reason. I wanted you alone." Zaid continued sulking.

Her mind raced through images of what she'd like him to do to her. She was melting on this chair.

Their food arrived in waves. First was a bite sized appetizer, then soup, then scallops, a sorbet, then steak. She'd never had this much food before, and everything looked great. She couldn't fully taste everything, though. Zaid's gaze affected her from her toes curling, to legs clenching, and her stunned taste buds. The chemistry between them ratcheted up a notch with every dish. By the time dessert arrived, Lauren's inhibitions had dissipated into nothing. She'd blame the wine, but they both knew it was just *them*.

There was something between them, something that felt like it had been forged through years of companionship. But that was impossible. They'd only just met. But she wanted to get to know him, play with him. She wanted him. She took a spoonful of ice cream, licked it then slowly dragged it out of her mouth.

"Tease." Zaid grinned.

"Is this okay?" She dragged a finger down her neck, letting her fingertips wander lower to graze the skin between her breasts.

"More than okay," Zaid replied. He leaned back and blatantly adjusted his pants.

They had leaned towards each other without thought. Being with him felt like the most natural thing in the world. Their mouths found each other. Their tongues tangled in a wet kiss.

His fingers found their way into her pants. "Goddamnit. You're so wet." He nuzzled into her neck and breathed in. "Come here. Straddle me."

"We can't do it here!" She gasped even as she scrambled to get on top of him. They moaned in unison when she nestled herself over him.

He cupped the back of her neck and claimed her lips. She was melting like butter on a very hot pancake. Lauren had never been this turned on before. He reciprocated each touch and sound tenfold. With every touch, she gained more confidence. She used to struggle with being stuck in her head. She had trouble just relaxing and simply feeling. But with him, she was different. Case in point: she was enthusiastically dry-humping him now.

He pulled away for a second. "No one will disturb us. Take me out, little rabbit."

Her fingers fumbled with his zipper while her remaining brain cells decided to tease him. "Is this what you were talking about when you reserved this place?"

"This wasn't part of my plan. I wanted to properly make love to you the first time. Take my time. On a bed."

"Do it here. Do everything here," she demanded, uncaring how she sounded. She was operating purely on instinct. Her mind filled with need. She slid down to her knees to have better access to him. His bulge distracted her, and she ended up caressing him through his pants.

"Jesus fucking Christ. Lauren, *please.*"

"What?"

"Take me out. Touch me. More, *please.*"

She licked her lips and pulled him out but only managed a couple of strokes before he stopped her.

"Fuck!" He held her wrists gently but firmly, chest heaving heavy-lidded eyes gazing right at her. He rasped out, "I'm sorry, rabbit. I think I overestimated myself." He touched her shirt. "Will you take this off for me?" After a microsecond of hesitation, she pulled off her shirt. "Lauren. You look absolutely breathtaking." He grazed his fingers over her shoulders almost reverently. His hands traveled downwards, lightly brushing over the curves of her breasts, and lower to her ribs, making her suck in a breath.

"Take this off too." She tugged at the lapels of his shirt.

He grinned almost shyly before slowly undoing his shirt. Button by agonizing button, he took his time.

Her mouth dried up as she studied the planes of his body. She'd never been good at drawing bodies or at sculpting. But she suddenly had the urge to learn. He was a masterpiece. He was Michelangelo's 'David', defined by sinewy muscles that rippled with every movement. There were a few scars on the contours of his chest and abdomen, but the imperfections made him even more perfect.

She must have mumbled it out loud because he suddenly said, "Baby, you're the one who is a work of art."

He gently pushed her shoulders until she laid her back on the table. His hands found their way over his body in fearless and joyful exploration.

She sighed in bliss and wrapped herself around him, knotting her hands and legs around his shoulders and hips. She tried to pull away but he growled and held her thighs in place. "Fair warning, little rabbit. There's no backing away now. You and I are well and truly tied together."

She blinked in surprise. "We're not—"

He didn't let her finish her sentence. "Not yet, but little rabbit, everything else is just semantics. In here," he thumped his chest, "where it matters, we're already tied together."

Something in Lauren clicked into place. His words made more sense than anything else in her life. She'd felt like she'd been adrift for so long in the vast ocean of life, and suddenly she was *here* with her person. It was like everything that had happened led her here and it was all meant to be.

He must've seen the realization in her eyes because the next few moments were spent in a flurry of tearing off each other's clothes. He bent down and licked her core.

"No," she keened. "I want to come with you!"

"You're so ready for me, Lauren. Can I put it in?"

She wiggled. "I want to put the condom on you."

He moaned, nodded, and maneuvered their bodies so she could easily reach him. That was all the encouragement she needed.

She wrapped her hands around him.

She could feel him losing control as she stroked him with both hands.

He let out another throaty groan. "I can't take much more of this, little rabbit," he complained. "I need to be inside you."

As he pulsed in her hold, precum leaking from the tip of his shaft, she took the condom packet he'd laid beside them. She slowly rolled it over his length. He pulled her up and hoisted her on the table. The care he put into arranging her—she'd just become the main course. She felt his smooth thick cock fill her up.

"Christ, you feel so good! You're made for me, little rabbit."

She nodded, words failing her because it was perfect. He was perfect. There was no need for reshuffling or trial and error. This wasn't a couple's clumsy first time. This was an awakening. They just fit.

He entered her slowly, not stopping until he reached the hilt. She'd never felt so full, so complete. She loved the way he was stretching her. But then...

"What are you waiting for?" she moaned the complaint.

He chuckled, which annoyed her even more. "Just making sure you're ready for me, sweetheart."

Impatient, she moved against him. Her fingers dug into his back. If he wasn't going to help, she was going to ride him to oblivion herself. And god, did it feel good!

"Okay, I get it," he half-laughed half-moaned as she bounced her ass against him. "You get a few more seconds before I take over sweetheart." That was exactly what she wanted. He started pumping his hips. Her rhythm faltered and she saw stars. She lost the next few minutes to pure pleasure as they moved together.

"Fuck, You are going to be the death of me. Tell me you're close, baby," he huffed in between pants.

"I'm close," she choked out.

He flipped her over. She was expecting and looking forward to him railing her. But their eyes locked together, and time slowed to a crawl.

He started moving against her, all the while keeping eye contact. They stared at each other as if they could see straight to the depths of each other's soul all the while climbing to their peaks together. Each step, together. Each thrust, together. Her whine as she came echoed all around them. She would've been embarrassed if it wasn't for his voice that was louder than hers as he moaned his orgasm with her.

CHAPTER III

Zaid

Zaid's head was up in the clouds despite the very serious meeting he was in with Dominic Miranda, his boss and the head of the family that ruled over the Vatan Valley underground. He'd started working for the family since he was a young boy. Zaid would willingly and proudly take a bullet to the heart for Dom. He almost did one time, but Dom had rolled them both out of harm's away. He'd berated him right after the altercation. "What was the point of living if we only glorified death?"

Zaid had joked he was born to be Dom's right hand man. Dom hated his reply. So naturally, whenever Dom did something that annoyed Zaid, he'd repeat the joke over and over for the rest of the day.

"Sotto is trying to break into our territory." Dominic Miranda leaned back in his chair, fingers steepled in front of him. Anger radiated off of him. "They're peddling guns to all the other groups."

Yup. He was definitely a little too chipper considering the main topic of their meeting.

"Do you want me to organize an operation against the Sottos?" It would be messy. It would mean war.

"Not yet." Dom shook his head once.

This was part of a complicated power play. Zaid had hoped Sotto was smarter than this. But, of course, he was too proud. Such was the downfall of most men in his stature.

Sotto used to be the biggest underground group until the Miranda family rose to power. It happened so quickly and it was all because Dom had stepped up to lead. From the outside, it would seem that Dom was too young, too green. But every single member of the Miranda clan respected him.

Zaid knew that was not an easy feat. He might not be a Miranda by name, but he had grown up well entrenched in the clan. The Cervantes family had long been adopted by the Mirandas ever since his great-grandfather had joined the organization.

Sotto was probably offended that a 'boy' half his age was leading a group that was in charge of

Vatan Valley, one of the most influential cities in the country. Sotto had been wanting to expand his territory. He probably thought Dom was an easy target. So now he was trying to engage Dom into a pissing contest.

It was a monumental mistake. They were already pissed at one of his subsidiaries and currently working on taking the rat out. Sottos were old-school crime lords. Meanwhile, Dom was cleaning up their operations—not quite legal, but with much more respect for life.

"We could block his operations from our city. The problem is: there is a demand."

Zaid nodded. "If we control the supply, there won't be much of a problem." Dodger came to mind. "My cousin deals with weapons."

"Dodger?" Dom raised an eyebrow.

He pursed his lips. "His father is the black sheep of the Cervantes family, but Dodge's all right and that business is all him."

"If you vouch for him, that's good enough for me. Can we contact him? We might as well start overseeing the operations ourselves."

"Sure." This was the safest way to ensure their territory. Money wouldn't hurt. It was just a byproduct. Dom was wearing a luxury suit he'd had tailored to fit him perfectly. Zaid was in no position to say anything. After all, his suit was of the same brand and tailored as well.

Dom leaned forward and unlocked his fingers. That signaled the business talk was over. But before Zaid could relax further into his seat, Dom narrowed his eyes at Zaid. "By the way… how was your mini excursion yesterday?" Dominic's hawk eyes grazed over every millimeter of his face.

"It went by quick. Seems like a quiet neighborhood, but Diez will do a more thorough sweep tomorrow."

"Then you took a personal leave for the rest of the day."

"Yes. *Personal*." He shouldn't have said that. Now he sounded like an overly defensive ass.

Dom's lips spread into a knowing smirk. "That your way of telling me it's none of my business?"

He contemplated staying silent. But since Dom already knew something was up anyway, he might as well lean into it. "Depends. Are you going to tell me what's up with you and Soph?"

"Soph? Since when have you two become so close that you're giving her a nickname?" Dom growled.

Zaid laughed. "I heard other people call her 'Soph'."

"Stop saying it. It's only Nine who calls her that."

"Fine. Sophie, then."

"It's Ms. Damas to you!" Dom visibly bristled. "Better yet just don't address her. Don't talk about her! Or even think about her!"

Zaid shook his head. "You're as crazy as my great-grandfather over my great-grandma. Not that I can blame you." Zaid looked down at his nails, making a show of buffing them on his lapels. "I found my one yesterday."

"Ah." Dom didn't laugh or question his statement. "Did you get married?"

It was a fair question. Dom knew about the Cervantes men. They didn't fall in love. They *mated*. There was no other word for it. Zaid's great-great-grandfather married his great-great-grandmother the same afternoon they met. They were both eighteen. Same with his grandpa and dad. His father waited a week after meeting his mother, and he was still getting teased for it during reunions even when everyone knew he'd only allowed the delay because Zaid's mom wanted time to prepare a grand wedding.

At thirty-five, Zaid was starting to worry he didn't have a soulmate. He'd been bouncing around, feeling nothing when his father, grandfather, and great-grandfather found theirs before they reached twenty-five. His great-great-grandfather found his mate when he was a damn kid and it was like a fucking soap opera. Compared to that, Zaid's situation was pretty straightforward.

"There was a complication. I took care of it, but I have a feeling he's going to come back."

"Why not just kill this complication?" Dom asked, sounding genuinely perplexed.

"Didn't want to scare off my girl."

Dom hummed, his eyes drifting to the door where his secretary sat on the other side of the wall. His voice was a rumble when he asked, "Need help?"

"No." Like hell was Dom going anywhere near his Lauren. She was *his*.

"I get the feeling that you're going to be busy in the coming days."

Zaid replied with a noncommittal shrug. He didn't have a concrete plan yet, but the goal was to get his little rabbit to willingly walk into his trap. He was already diverging from their family tradition by waiting, but no Cervantes had ever gotten divorced. Once she was with him, it was for life.

CHAPTER IV

Lauren

Zaid: Good morning, little rabbit. Did you receive the flowers?
Lauren: Good morning. Yes, they are lovely. How did you?
Zaid: I have my ways.

Three days had passed and Zaid texted her every day since their encounter. She was trying to keep it casual and not overthink it. She thought it was a one-night stand kind of arrangement, but Zaid kept surprising her. He sent her flowers today as well. She found it on her kitchen counter when she woke up, which was kind of creepy but impressive at the same time. His note read: 'You have a new stalker now', which made her inadvertently laugh.

It was inappropriate and involuntary. She almost choked on her own saliva once the sound escaped her throat.

Shaking her head, she took out her phone and started typing.

Lauren: I just read the note.
Zaid: I was going to write 'I love you', but I thought that might scare you.

Her lips quirked. She was about to reply when she saw that he was typing a new message.

Zaid: I'll say it again when you're ready. I'll make an event out of it. Be ready soon.
Lauren: How about asking me out on a proper date first? Or would you prefer to remain my stalker?
Zaid: I can be anything and everything you want to be, little rabbit.

She rolled her eyes, but she clenched her legs together despite herself. And she'd never thought she'd be joking about this ever.

However, she couldn't help but notice his lack of initiative in asking her out. Oh well, it was his loss. After all, today was one of her rare self-imposed rest days. As a full-time freelancer, these were sacred to her. She'd already planned out her day. She was going to go back to sleep after ordering takeout. Later, she was going to clean the house, take Bonnie out for a walk, and then have a movie night by herself. She didn't need a man to have a fun relaxing day. She could take care of herself.

That night, she'd put on a fresh set of pajamas. She settled on her couch. It had been a productive day. Bonnie was huddled by herself in her dog bed, resting after Lauren had taken her out. The opening credits of Lauren's favorite comfort movie scrolled down the screen.

The microwave dinged, and she stood up to get her popcorn when she heard rustling from her room.

"Bonnie?" she called out softly. Somehow, she had a feeling that it wasn't her Bonnie who'd made the noise. Her heart raced. All internal alarms in her body started blaring, yelling at her to run.

Gerald stepped out from the shadows. She was ready to yell at him to get out, chew him out for daring to creep inside her house in the first place. She was a new woman. She had newfound courage and confidence thanks to Zaid. But then Gerald drew out a gun.

"What are you doing in my house?" Her voice was a lot steadier than she felt. Gerald followed her around, showing up in the most unexpected places. She'd even seen him watching her from across the street, but he'd never actually entered her home.

"What do you think?" he drawled out. "How dare you let another man touch you? Do you think you can do better than me? You think that guy can protect you?" He was waving the gun around like it was a pinwheel toy.

Lauren didn't say anything, not wanting to agitate him further, but he continued advancing toward her.

"I can see it in your eyes. You think I'm shit? You think I'm just going to let this happen?"

She frantically shook her head, but she could see it was all in vain. Gerald was officially stark raving mad.

"I can't let you go! I won't!" Surely now the police wouldn't be able to deny her claims. Too bad she'd probably be dead before she could report this.

She almost wanted to laugh. Maybe the crazy was contagious. Gerald drew nearer. She had nowhere to go. There was no one to help her.

Bonnie started barking. With bared teeth, her hind legs bent back, preparing to attack. Gerald shifted his aim to the growling pit bull.

"No!" Lauren screamed. Panicked, she shoved Gerald's chest, putting all of her weight on it. Because she caught him off guard, she was able to break free from his hold. He grabbed her. She dodged and turned to run, making a beeline to Bonnie, moving her legs as fast as she could. If she could reach Bonnie and the door, they might have a chance. Her head was yanked back. He'd grabbed her ponytail and pulled her. She screamed again.

A shot rang out. Lauren dropped to the floor with another scream. Bonnie was beside her. She grabbed her collar. Then a gun landed in front of her. Apparently, Gerald had dropped it. Hands shaking, she took the gun and pointed it at him.

This was the first time she'd held a gun. She hoped she was holding it properly.

"Good girl." Zaid's cool baritone echoed from a dark corner of the room. He emerged like a horseman of the apocalypse. She could feel the heat of his rage radiating off of him, and the full force of his wrath was directed at Gerald. "Your stupidity knows no bounds. I was going to kill you anyway, but your actions have expedited my plans." Zaid focused his attention back to her. "Don't worry little rabbit. I'll take care of this."

CHAPTER V

Zaid

He'd meant to surprise her with a date. The past few days he'd been busy with Sotto and the rat. Tonight was his first breath of fresh air. He'd been looking forward to spending the night cuddling with Lauren on her ratty sofa watching a movie together. He'd planned on watching her more than the movie, but that was beside the point.

He didn't expect to find a sliver of the darkness from his life to invade Lauren's home. Gerald might not be remotely connected to the mafia, and normally Zaid kept out of civilian's businesses, but this was his rabbit. Gerald had forcibly inserted himself into Lauren's life, and Zaid was going to permanently take him out of it. This asshole held not an ounce of honor—coming into his girl's home uninvited and scaring her in her safe space. He dared not think about what could have happened if he hadn't come.

Zaid kept his eyes trained on the asshole. He raised a hand, palms spread open, and signaled Lauren to keep calm and stand by. He was going to take care of this piece of shit. In a split second, he kicked Gerald on the knee. The piece of shit bent over. The moment he tried to stand back up, Zaid hit his nose with a hammer fist strike. In quick succession, he directed a punch to his liver. Gerald was down. But Zaid wasn't satisfied. Not one bit. Violence thrummed in his veins. The monster in him was roaring for blood. For death. No. *More*. He wanted a slow agonizing death for this piece of shit. He wanted to hear deafening cries of pain.

Lauren cowered in a corner, wrapping her arms around herself as if wanting to make herself appear as small as possible.

Zaid lost control. Gerald was still on the ground and Zaid unleashed the demon inside of him.

He kicked the asshole. Gerald screamed. It was music to his ears. Zaid kicked him repeatedly, savoring the cries of pain. He didn't give Gerald any space or time to recover. Zaid was not going to play fair, not when his girl was involved. When his whimpers faded away, Zaid leaned down and grabbed him by the hair. Zaid lifted him and drove the knife into Gerald's gut.

At first, Gerald thrashed, then he grunted. He managed to grab Zaid's shirt, but slowly his grip lost strength. He tumbled to the ground.

Zaid twisted the knife for good measure, only letting go when Gerald's chest stopped moving.

He swept his hair away from his face and turned to Lauren. She stared at Gerald. More specifically, her eyes were transfixed on the blood pooling around the dead body.

He kicked Gerald's lifeless body. She flinched, but he couldn't muster enough logical thought to feel sorry. He should have killed the asshole when he saw him in the park. It was his mistake. But never again.

He pulled his phone out and typed in a number. "Clean up." He recited out her address and dropped the call.

His attention snapped back to Lauren. His gut churned with a multitude of emotions. She was still in the corner, still shaking like a leaf.

He'd raise hell before he'd let anything like this happen to her again. He was going to have eyes on her at all times. He was going to be her personal security. His sun was going to rise and set with her.

He stalked towards her and put a handkerchief over her mouth. She was pliant and lost consciousness almost immediately. It was like she welcomed the quiet. It was like he gave her peace.

CHAPTER VI

Lauren

She regained consciousness to see thick metal strips molded into gothic swirls looming above her. She groaned and sat up. Bonnie was licking her cheek. Her head throbbed with the worst headache of her life. "Where am I?" she mumbled while subconsciously rubbing Bonnie's head. Their vehicle was crossing a vast expanse of what appeared like a perfectly manicured lawn. It looked more like vast plains that photographers would love to shoot and companies would love to scrawl their motto on.

"Did you have a good nap, little rabbit? Bonnie was such a good girl during the drive." Zald was beside her. She nodded groggily. The last thing she remembered was Gerald in her house. And then Zald showed up. And then... she gasped. "Gerald's dead."

Zaid's jaw hardened. "He won't bother you anymore. Nobody will," Zaid said through gritted teeth.

Lauren watched him warily, unable to gauge his mood. Weird. She wasn't scared of him. She'd been more scared of Gerald and he didn't even touch her… only showed up in the most unexpected and inappropriate places like her house. Oh god! He was gone. There will be no more phone calls filled with only raspy breaths, no more wondering if a phone call is a real person or it will be Gerald's raspy breathing. She could jog in peace, no more looking behind her back when she walked outside. He was dead… and Lauren felt nothing but freedom.

"You'll be staying in my house," Zaid suddenly announced. A beautiful luxurious bungalow lay ahead.

Huh. That peace only lasted a second. "Excuse me?" she bristled. Bonnie sat in attention at her feet, but she apparently already trusted Zaid enough that she didn't feel like she was in any danger.

"You're moving in with me," he repeated like it was nothing. Like he was describing the weather. It was an order he was expecting her to follow.

Lauren strove for calmness. "Don't you think we should talk about this?"

"No," he said simply.

"I'm not going to live with you," she said flatly.

He raised an eyebrow. "Where do you want to go? Because there's no way I'm letting you live in that apartment where an intruder got in!"

"I could stay in a hotel."

"Why would you have to? We're already here."

She wasn't able to do anything when he grabbed her wrist and pulled her out of the car.

His house exuded quiet luxury in its loudest form. There were no towers or pillars, no gold vases or molding. Instead, it sported a very sleek modern design that sprawled as if wanting to occupy the largest expanse of land possible. The materials used looked simple but one touch or an extra minute of closer inspection would expose expensive quality—the softest velvet, the smoothest marble, the intricate grain of wood. No expense had been spared for literally every detail.

Zaid's place was a mansion complete with a small army of men in suits with earpieces. If he'd said snipers were hiding in the trees, she would've believed him. It had never been more obvious that he was out of her league.

How the hell did she find herself in this position? With this man? Why would he even want her? Was this some kind of reality TV show?

An actual alpaca trotted around on his front lawn. She tugged on Bonnie's leash in reflex. If this wasn't a hallucination and a symptom she'd lost her mind, she was certainly losing it now.

He noticed her staring. "That's Maximus. My grandpa gave him to me when I was young after we visited a petting zoo, and I cried when we had to leave." He scratched the back of his neck, looking embarrassed. "I know. It's excessive. My grandpa had always been over the top. You'll see when you meet him. You'll get used to Maximums. He's more like a pet dog than anything else. He's also used to actual dogs because of Clyde."

Lauren took everything in, dazed and slightly scared but mostly confused. Why did he take her here? This appeared to be his sanctuary.

They climbed up the stairs, flanked by two guards in suits. Lauren let Zaid usher her into a room. He locked the door behind her, leaving the two guards outside.

Her anxiety kicked in. An image flashed in her head, of him hovering over her, eyes warm and worried, a hanky in his hand. She remembered a floral scent with a strong metallic undertone.

"What did you do? Did you drug me?"

"It was the easiest way to get you here." He didn't answer her question and that was answer enough.

"Again. *Why?*"

"You are in danger. You need someone to protect you. I will step in for the job."

"You don't have to keep me in your *home.*"

"You will stay *here.* With *me.* End of story." He ran a frustrated hand through his hair. "Why are you fighting me on this? I will take care of you. I need you by my side at all times so I can protect you."

Her heart skipped a beat and a large part of her annoyance melted away. It felt nice, having someone who insisted on taking care of her when she'd always had to do everything herself.

Stop it, she quickly berated herself. He'd spoken like he'd made up his mind and that was all that mattered. He'd also sounded extremely protective like he actually loved her. That was just… crazy. It couldn't be true. This whole scenario was crazy and while she could easily let herself be swept away, apparently, she was the only voice of reason left. Even Bonnie had laid on her belly and was now snoring in the corner.

Lauren fought against her hormones. She'd be damned if she let the nerves in her groin area overtake her thinking facilities.

"So the bottom line is I have no say in my living arrangements?"

"You're not a prisoner here. You will be fed and clothed. You can roam around the grounds and in the house except the west wing."

"What's in the west wing?"

"My dungeon."

She couldn't tell if he was joking or not. "Where will I sleep?"

He ground his teeth together. "This is our room. I had your things already set up."

Our room.

She looked to the right and saw that Bonnie had slept next to her bags. The closet was half open and some of her clothes were peaking out. More importantly, her tablet and computer were sitting on a desk beside her measly set of bags.

"This set-up is temporary. Once you've seen all the rooms and decided which one you want as your office, I'll have all your tech moved there."

She pointed at the unfamiliar tablet. "I only have one iPad."

"That's the latest model. All your files have been synched. I'll get you the latest drawing tablet as well. They just didn't have stock right now. The iMac will be coming in tomorrow."

She was speechless. She felt like she was in a dream. He had all her things delivered and arranged in here. She didn't need to ask. That was sweet, right? He even bought her the latest iPad and pencil. Hers was already beat up and worn out. She'd planned on upgrading once she could fit it into her budget, but… here they were.

Someone knocked on the door. Zaid opened it and a tall man with dark hair and intense eyes walked in. "Diez will be looking after you when I need to attend to business."

Lauren's blood pressure rose up so fast that her ears rang. "I can take care of myself!"

"If you need anything, approach him. You can trust him," Zaid said dismissively.

He wasn't listening to her. She imagined this 'conversation' would have gone the same way if she'd been talking to a brick with pre-recorded answers. She was pissed at herself for being attracted to a brick. "And what? You're giving me your tenth guy??" she mumbled.

"Actually, I was born in October," Diez cut in. She just blinked. Diez smirked then winked. "I kept the name because I've been told I'm ten out of ten in bed."

Lauren rolled her eyes so hard she saw the back of her skull.

She heard a slap. When he looked at back at the two men. Diez was biting back a grin and rubbing the side of his head.

"Flirt with her again and I'll cut off all your appendages," Zaid growled.

"Well noted," Diez replied. He didn't seem all that scared of Zaid either. He looked amused and that was pissing Zaid off even more.

"You can leave now."

"I'll stand guard outside."

"I don't need a bodyguard," she tried again.

"Always knock before entering. Use the emergency code during any hint of danger."

Diez chuckled. "Like you said, Z. You can trust me."

"Excuse me! Can you two not hear me?" She hated that she was now properly whining. She was painfully aware of how much she'd been more afraid of Gerald than Zaid. With Zaid, she was more annoyed than scared even when she'd seen how ruthless he could be. A headache was forming right smack dab in the middle of her forehead.

Diez stepped out, leaving Lauren and Zaid alone in the room again. He took one glance at her and said, "Sleep. You're exhausted."

"Is this how it's going to be between us? You're just going to ignore everything I say?"

"Do I need to drug you again?"

"Don't you dare!"

"Lauren, love." His tone was laced with gravity. "I'll do worse things than drug you if it ensures your safety." He put a hand into his pocket as if getting a drug.

Lauren made the snap decision to jump into the bed.

"Rest, little rabbit. You've had a long day."

He slammed the door just in time to block the bottle of water on the side table that she threw at his head. She was seething. But the moment she laid her head on the pillow, she promptly fell asleep.

Lauren stirred awake. She knew immediately she wasn't in her own bed because she was so warm and comfortable. The memories came in waves starting with the best one-night stand of her life, to Gerald and death, to finding herself in Zaid's home. She'd just been ushered from one prison to another. Resentment and anger bubbled up her gut.

If they thought she was just going to be some meek prisoner, they'd severely underestimated her. Then again, she couldn't run around in a rampage. That was a surefire way to end up tied to a chair. She needed to be smart, bid her time, and plan so she could utilize the element of surprise. That didn't mean she had to be nice to them. She pouted and sulked, resolving not to answer any questions and to make things as hard as she could for them, without getting herself killed.

She stood up and looked over to Bonnie. She wasn't there. She bolted upright. Lauren ran to the door. There was a fingerprint panel and without thinking, she tried scanning her thumb on it. The door opened, and she was ready to run out, only to find her beloved pittie belly up in front of a crouching Diez, receiving belly rubs. Lauren was lightheaded with relief. Bonnie didn't even acknowledge her. The little traitor.

"Do you need anything?" Diez asked.

Lauren's heart was still pounding in her chest from too much adrenaline. She was also very much annoyed at Bonnie, the little traitor, and Diez, for being… here? For existing? This house and this situation was really messing with her head.

"Just tell me if you need anything. Clothes or toiletries. We could get them to you."

She resolutely ignored him, turning her head to the side.

"Hungry?"

She shook her head, but her stomach growled in agreement. Diez chuckled and gestured for her to follow. "To the kitchen! Just as well, Lola Bella had been itching to meet you."

Lauren had to sprint a little to keep up with Diez long strides. Behind her she could hear the click of claws on the tiles. Bonnie and Clyde. She wasn't sure if they were following her or Diez, but she threw them a smile. These two furry potential-traitors were too cute to be really mad at. "Lola? Your grandmother works here?"

"Not by blood, but as long as you live here she's everyone's granny! And don't let her catch you talking about what she does here as 'work'." Diez led her to the lower floor. Diez knocked on the door, tapping a specific rhythm like he did this multiple times a day every single day. "Welcome to The Kitchen!" He opened the door with a flourish, and she understood why he'd said that with a capital 'T' and a capital 'K'. From the outside, it looked like any other room in the house, but once the double doors opened, the scents that greeted her were divine! The promise of delicious food.

"Lola Bella, I have a surprise for you!" Diez announced. The dogs ran inside going straight to a row of glass containers containing different kinds of cereals and cookies.

"What surprise? You rascals come in here like clockwork for the cookies!" the older woman standing in front of the cooktop grumbled. She turned around and her gaze landed on Lauren, a bright smile spread across her face. "You must be Lauren! What a pretty little thing you are!" She wiped her hands on her apron and walked over to Lauren with open arms. "I knew Zaid would chose well!"

Lauren bent down and let herself be enveloped in the warmest hug she'd ever experienced. Lola Bella only reached Lauren's shoulders. She almost looked like a cartoon character with her completely white curly hair that was determined to escape the tiny chef's hat on her head.

"That hat is adorable," she breathed out as Lola Bella let her go.

Diez blew out a soft amused laugh but didn't say anything else. He ambled to the corner where there were jars filled with a variety of cookies. He was definitely a regular in The Kitchen. He bent over and opened a smaller container with a handwritten label: 'dog treats'. So this was why these two rascals ran in like they owned the place.

"Thank you, dear." Lola Bella fluffed her hair. "I drew it out with exact measurements, and had it custom-made."

"It suits you," Lauren said, relieved that she hadn't offended anybody.

"Oh, you're such a sweetheart! I'm glad you came to visit!" Lola Bella let out a jolly belly laugh. "Who am I kidding? I was going to *insist* on meeting the lady of the house!"

Lauren shook her head, flustered. "I'm not–"

A plate appeared on Lauren's hand and Lola Bella hobbled to the large island and started taking samples of food and putting it on her plate. "I don't know yet what you like, so try a little bit of anything."

Lauren felt her tummy start to complain with hunger. Before it could embarrass her by growling again, she started eating everything. It wasn't a hardship because everything smelled and tasted amazing.

Lola Bella watched with a smile. "You have a healthy appetite. I'm glad." It felt like her plate was refilling by itself, but Lauren was not complaining. "Ah! How could I forget? How do you like your coffee, dear?"

"Do you have milk and sugar?"

"Of course! You're welcome to the kitchen whenever you're hungry or in need of female company. I'll gladly fix you something up."

Lauren shook her head. "I'll become fat."

Lola Bella gasped indignantly. "Nonsense! My darling girl, you have curves in all the right places!"

"Don't let Zaid hear you call yourself fat," Diez warned through a mouthful of cookies.

Lauren made a face, looking back and forth at a kind granny's soft face and a tall brute's scarred mug. Both faces were full of reprimand. "Um.. I *am* fat."

Diez rolled his eyes. "Don't say I didn't warn you. You're Zaid's girl. Nobody can talk down to you, not even you."

Lauren just rolled her eyes. *Bring it on.* She was sure she could deal with whatever Zaid dished out. In fact, she couldn't wait to fight with him again.

✱ ✱ ✱

Except seven days had passed and she heard not a peep out of Zaid. It was like the man had disappeared. She couldn't bring herself to ask Diez about him, not wanting to look needy. But she had reached the end of her rope.

The house was perfect. Lola Bella's food was great. In here, she could work without distractions. She was already used to Maximus walking around and peering into windows. There was a pool she'd already used, wearing a swimsuit that magically appeared on the bed. She had everything she could ever need. Even Bonnie was enamored by the place. Her traitor dog had taken to roaming and running around with her new boyfriend while conveniently ignoring her most of the day.

Everything was great.

But still this was *not* her home. If she had to leave her old apartment, then she needed to find a new place to move into. She needed to find her new normal. Ideally, before she got too used to this mansion.

She set out to hunt Zaid down. The first step would be to get Zaid's location out of Diez.

"He's working out. Basement." That was easier than expected. Diez didn't spare her a glance. "Do me a favor. Knock some sense into his thick mug. People have been in and out of this house and we've been busy as hell, but working with him has been worse than working for Satan the past week." He shot her a dark look. "I wonder why." Diez's last sentence dripped with sarcasm.

She took that as permission to go to Zaid. "I'll do my best to avenge you."

He smirked. "Stop. You'll get me killed."

Lauren was already walking away. Bonnie ambled next to her. It was a miracle her dog decided to spend time with her. Her dog had abandoned her and spent her days if not with Clyde, then with Diez. Lauren rolled her eyes as Bonnie stepped closer to her, still very much salty that every morning Bonnie chose Diez over her. Diez had to have been sharing Lola Bella's treats with her. Sighing, she patted Bonnie's side, resigned to settle for the crumbs of her dog's affection.

The entrance to the basement was in the forbidden west wing. Diez had pointed it out to her offhandedly because it was near the pool.

She couldn't care less if she was walking onto cursed ground. She was going to talk to Zaid today. They'd probably fight and yell. He could set the house on fire with his wrath for all she cared. They were going to hash everything out *today*.

The lights dimmed as she descended the stairs to get to the basement. Lauren's heart started to pound. She could hear a soundtrack of ominous beats playing, reminiscent of horror movies. Her imagination ran wild with images of a classy dungeon. Dark marble floors and walls. It would be relatively easy to clean. He'd find a way to soundproof it. A series of manacles hung on the wall in even intervals. There would be strategically placed track spotlights. She hit the landing and was greeted by a glass partition. Zaid was inside it, practicing some kind of martial arts routine.

Her dark mood dissipated, transforming into a cloud of pheromones.

He was wearing dark gray sweatpants and nothing else. He went through a series of moves, moving so smoothly that it was obvious he'd done it thousands of times before. His body moved automatically like it was second nature. He looked like he was concentrating on his routine. Meanwhile she was concentrating on the muscles on his back, mesmerized by the way they flexed. She barely registered that she'd reached an actual gym and not a dungeon. Beads of sweat rolled down his abs and she wondered what it would feel like to lick them off. Her gaze traveled lower to the bulge below his waistband. Her mouth watered. She probably looked like Bonnie with her tongue lolling out the side of her mouth.

She jumped when he suddenly addressed her. "You need anything?"

"I wasn't looking," she squeaked. She was a horrible liar. He lifted a brow but thankfully didn't push. She looked around and noted that the overall aesthetic of his personal gym was, as expected, dark and modern, consistent with the rest of the house.

"I can teach you basic moves."

It was then that Lauren remembered why she came. She exploded. "How dare you!"

"What?" He had the gall to look confused. "I've left you alone!"

"Exactly! You've brought me here, kept me captive, and then you just disappear!"

"Captive!" Zaid spit out. "You're free in here! Do what you want. I'd say you have more freedom here than you did back in your dingy apartment. Besides, considering the way you reacted when I brought you in, I thought you'd like to be given space."

"You abandoned me!" Lauren's shriek rendered them both speechless.

Zaid blinked slowly. The realization dawned on both of them at the same time—what was making her angry, more than the abduction, was Zaid's absence. That first night she'd been ready to yell her head off, to scream at him until he was deaf. But the man had completely abandoned her. She hadn't seen a hair on his head since their first fight. And she was hurt. He claimed to care about her. Liar. If he really cared about her, where did he go?

"You've been a bad girl."

"*Excuse me?*" She refused to be swayed by *that tone.*

"Diez told me what you said when you visited the kitchen."

"That big-mouthed traitor," she grumbled in full sulk.

"He's one of my men, rabbit. He's doing his job. And you. You need a lesson. I'm sorry I've been a horrible host, little rabbit," Zaid purred. "I've been neglecting you haven't I?" He prowled towards her and caged her between his body and the table behind her. "We need to remedy that right now."

He cupped her ass and lifted, placing her on the table. Zaid hooked her legs on his arms and pulled. Lauren fell back, wide eyes and locked on his face. He pulled off his shirt in one smooth motion. He left his sweatpants hanging low on his hips. His straining cock was perfectly outlined under the gray fabric. Lauren's mouth watered at the sight. "Let me take care of you, love."

Her core clenched in response. Her eyes roamed over the planes of his torso. It was impossible not to admire how perfectly sculpted his body was. Legs quivering, she nodded.

He slid his hands up her thighs and pulled her panties off. His fingers ran back down to her calves and pushed her legs open wider. Before her brain could register an ounce of shyness, his face was between her thighs. His tongue caressed her clit. She whimpered and lifted her hips. He leaned back and with amazing control, glided the tip of his tongue over her, teasing her. When his finger entered her, curving, and stroking, she almost fell apart.

"Oh my god, Zaid!" She was going to come. *I can't be.* It was too fast. But it made sense. Everything he did made her climb and soar with roaring intensity. Before she knew it, she was coming and doubling over.

When her body finally calmed down and stopped convulsing, Zaid was watching over her with a smug smile, looking so proud of himself that it made her smile. She shook her head, trying to clear it. There was no way she was going to just take all

"Wow..." she breathed out. He was huge, almost intimidating with visible veins wrapped around its length.

Zaid chuckled. "That's all for you, little rabbit. I've never been this hard... only for you. Can you handle it?"

Instead of saying anything, she wrapped both hands around him. She took the swollen head in her mouth.

"Fuck. Can I?" He cupped the back of her neck.

God yes! She would've said 'please' except her mouth was busy. She nodded.

He took a fistful of her hair and sank deep *deep* into her mouth. She loved it. "Fuck, fuck fuck. This is... I couldn't have imagined how... god! You're taking me so deep. You're doing so well. My little rabbit is... *fuck*... You're the best I've ever had. The best on fucking earth."

Tears prickled the back of her eyes, but she loved this. She tightened her fingers and pumped him as he ground against her mouth. She savored the feel of his smooth engorged cock against her tongue and the walls of mouth. He was going to fill her up so good. She felt her legs trembling and grasped the back of his thighs tighter. He was unraveling for her, because of her. His groans and gasps made her hungrier and hotter. The noises he was eliciting out of her made her wetter. He was close. She could feel it. She kept her rhythm, sucking harder.

"Shit!" It was a sharp shout. He drew himself out of her. "You liked that?"

She smiled at him, knowing she probably looked like a mess, but also, based from the reverence that shone on his face, that he loved what she did. "Yes."

"Not going to come in your mouth. On your back, baby. I want to watch your face while you beg." He supported her as she leaned into position. "You ready for me?" She nodded. He took out a condom and put it on. He tugged her closer to him for a better fit. "Look at me when I'm fucking you, little rabbit." Her eyes locked with his. "Such a good girl. You're dripping wet from sucking me off? God, you're fucking perfect." He entered her with one thrust, hitting home, making her gasp. She cried out as he expertly rolled his lips. He rocked into her and she ground back.

"Zaid!"

"You want to come?"

"Yes!"

"Not yet. Hold it for me, little rabbit." She shook her head. Her hips bucking against his, her body mindlessly chasing the promise of pleasure. Zaid slowed his thrusts. She met his every push and their every movement brought her closer. He was in complete control, watching her face closely. "Soon, baby. Just... don't want to draw this out longer? Fuck the whole day? The whole week. It's so good for me, baby. So fucking good. I'd fuck you forever if I could. I don't want to stop. Little rabbit... my little rabbit..." He moaned.

She didn't have enough brain power left to reply. All she could do was writhe beneath him, accept what he gave, while reaching for more. She was so close that she felt like a single pulsing nerve whose only purpose was pleasure. His and hers. This was heaven with the promise of more. Anything he wanted she'd give it to him. Because she knew everything he did would be tenfold for her. She was ruined. He had ruined her. Forever? That didn't seem enough. Her soul would yearn for him in this life and the next, for all eternity.

"Oh no, baby... I think you're on the absolute brink. That's okay. Are you ready?" She gasped and whined. "I'll take that as a yes." He gave her two hard thrusts that threw her over the edge. Whimpering and losing her mind, her hands scrambled for something to hold onto. Zaid reached out for her and intertwined their fingers. He continued their slow dance until she came over and over again. There was no limit when she was with him.

She was limp by the time they were done. She mumbled a complaint when he left her side, but then he came back with a warm wet towel and wiped her clean. She didn't have the energy to be shy and protest.

"Such a good little rabbit," he said as he dropped a kiss on her head.

She turned and met his gaze. His eyes glistened with strong emotion, something that she couldn't name. It made her eyes tear up. Maybe now he'd be more receptive and actually listen to her. "About my house…"

"What about it?" His voice rose, and he glowered over her.

And just like that all the gooeyness of the moment dissipated. After sex high wasn't enough to help her get through him. She pouted. Maybe she was the only one who thought the experience was earth-shattering. Maybe it was nothing to him. She couldn't believe she thought he *felt* for her. "I want to go back to my house!"

"Why?!"

"It's my house!"

"This is your house too!"

She huffed. It was remarkable how quickly he flipped from sexy partner to annoying captor. There was no talking sense to him. She made a swift about-face and started walking away.

"I meant what I said! You can visit me here every day. I'll teach you some moves." Zaid called out. Lauren wanted to turn around and slap the side of his head, but she didn't. She didn't want him to see how red her face had become.

CHAPTER VII

Zaid

The next day, Zaid headed to the office for his weekly meeting with Dom. The Miranda Tower housed their legitimate businesses. They hadn't completely let go of the old ways, Dom had simply chosen to conduct those activities elsewhere. It was a conscious effort and a recent decree from Dom. The times were changing and Dom said their organization had to change with it. Or maybe he kept the tower blood-free because Sophie was here. Zaid grinned at the thought.

Half of the floor was Dom's penthouse office. The rest of the floor were for essential personnel, a kitchen, and other spaces needed to make work more convenient. Most of the time only his secretary was in here with him. 'Essential personnel' was synonymous to 'Sophie'.

She sat in her desk a few feet away from Dom, waving Zaid in with a smile. He smiled back while Dom huffed in disapproval.

"Sophie could you leave us for minute?"

Zaid nodded at her to another one of Dom's huffs. Once she was out of the room, he raised an eyebrow at Dom. "How ever are you going to keep all the information without your secretary?"

Dom just glared at him.

"How long are you going to try and keep her in the dark? Don't you trust her?" He bit back a smile, waiting for Dom to react. He knew Dom trusted Sophie almost as much as he trusted him.

As expected, Dom tensed. He shot Zaid a glare with the fury of a thousand suns. Zaid barely refrained from laughing. But he couldn't help the big shit-eating grin that spread on his face. "It's for her safety," Dom growled.

Zaid rolled his eyes. "It's not that. You know we can keep her safe. Besides, do you really think she doesn't know what we do?"

"Any news on the rat running an operation under our noses?" Okayyy... Apparently, Dom was done discussing his secretary with him.

Fine. Zaid plopped down into one of Dom's leather visitor chairs. "Arrogant son of a bitch. Thinks he can take you on."

Dom took a slow sip of his coffee, eyes darkening. "How very stupid."

Zaid sighed. What could have easily been handled under the radar was threatening to become a spectacle. "He knows we're hunting him. It's going to make him careless."

"Sounds like he's going to get himself killed soon enough." Zaid had to agree. "More importantly, I'm wondering why I still haven't received an invitation to your wedding."

Apparently Dom didn't want to talk about Sophie, but didn't have a problem talking about Zaid's private life. "What makes you think you're invited?" Zaid grumbled.

"You're crabby. Don't tell me the honeymoon phase is over?"

Zaid sighed. "We're not there yet."

Dom's eyebrows furrowed. "Huh. Hasn't it been a little over a week since you met? I thought overnight marriages ran in your family."

Zaid wanted to punch Dom's nose off, but that would only prove his 'crabbiness'. Hearing all these things out loud only heightened his frustration. He should be in their bed right now. He should be spending all his nights with her, not sleeping in the guestroom. "At least, she's in my house," Zaid grumbled under his breath.

Dom's brows shot up. "She moved in?"

Zaid ground his teeth together. "I brought her in."

The brows settled back down. "Ah, you're holding her hostage," Dom said dryly.

Zaid gritted his teeth. "She's a valued guest in my home."

"If you don't know what's wrong with this situation, I don't think I can help you."

Zaid didn't reply. Everything was wrong. It wasn't his home. It was *theirs*. Lauren wasn't a guest. She was his *mate*. She was supposed to be his wife.

Sophie walked into their conversation. "Some details regarding your next meeting have changed." She stopped in her tracks, took one look at their faces, and rolled her eyes. "Did you ask me to leave so you could discuss girl problems?"

"Zaid's got girl problems. I don't have a girlfriend," Dom replied almost defensively.

"Maybe you should get one. She could probably help you get that stick out of your ass," Sophie replied coolly.

Zaid's lips twitched despite himself.

"Don't you dare laugh." Dom pointed at him. "Your woman is not even talking to you."

"She's just being stubborn."

She snorted loudly.

"What?" Zaid narrowed his eyes at her.

"Your last statement just underscored both of y'all problems! Y'all act like you know what's best for women, completely disregarding what we want. We're not stupid." She let out a frustrated sound and glared at Dom.

"We know you're not stupid!" Dom protested.

"We can make our own decisions! Figure things out for ourselves!" She put her hand on her hips and took a step closer to him.

"I know that!" Dom growled, leaning forward.

The sharp ring of Zaid's phone cut through their conversation. His screen lit up with his grandpa's name. "Excuse me," he mumbled, shaking his head as Dom and Sophie promptly continued bickering. They got off yelling at each other. At this point, they were practically tearing each other's clothes off. If only they were honest to themselves and each other, they'd be shoving their tongues down each other's throats. He walked away in disgust.

The moment he put the phone to his ear, he heard his grandpa's usual greeting. "Z."

"'Lo. Everything okay?"

"I'm still alive and kicking if that's what you're asking." Zaid could hear his grandpa rolling his eyes. "I heard you're shacking up with a girl." Damn nosy family. Lola Bella must've told everyone who had ears about Lauren. "Is she the one?"

"Yes."

"Then what are you waiting for? My death? I want to meet my great-grandkids, apo. I thought your father was bad. Back in my day…"

"I know 'Lo. I'm working on it."

"Are you? Do you need pointers?"

"I've told you kidnapping is frowned upon."

His grandpa scoffed. "I don't understand how and why you're in this situation. If it were me, I would be going crazy." He rasped out a dramatic sigh. "I've been told this is not the proper way to treat a lady. Claim her or let her go. If your great-grandfather was still alive, he would've already disowned you."

That made Zaid's stomach fold over itself. What could he say to that? "You'll be the first to know when we decide to get married."

"Don't bother! I want great-grandkids, apo!"

"'Lo, believe me, we want the same thing."

His grandpa huffed out a breath. "I called today hoping you have favorable news."

"You called to pressure me into committing crime so you can get great-grandkids earlier."

"Actually, I called to express my disappointment. I expected better from you."

"Mission accomplished. Disappointment well noted."

"Good. I need to go my boy. I hope the next time we talk you're, at the very least, married."

Zaid pinched the bridge of his nose. "Yes, 'Lo."

✳ ✳ ✳

Today was a weird day full of feelings that resembled guilt. Zaid was under no delusion that he was going to heaven. He was fine with that. He lived the way he lived. He did what he did and that was just the way it was. But today he felt something close to guilt, and it bothered him.

Coming home, Zaid thought he would finally be able to relax. He'd spent the whole day at the office where Sophie constantly lectured him.

Diez was waiting for him and he acknowledged him with a nod. Diez fell into step with him.

"She's in her room. Sleeping, I think." Disappointment sank deep in his gut. He was hoping she'd visit him again at the gym.

Diez cleared his throat. Zaid tilted his head in his friend's direction, curious and impatient. Diez was looking everywhere but him. He was obviously itching to tell him something. "She spends most of her time in her room."

Zaid was exhausted. He had zero patience. He wanted to see his little rabbit. He missed her.

"Spit it out, Diez."

"She'd been uhh crabby? Sad? I don't know. She said she wanted to go out. That might be good for her. If you like, I can organize an outing with proper security and make sure she's safe."

Zaid stopped in his tracks. An entire day's worth of bad mood descended on him. "Who are you to say what is good for *my girl*?" he growled.

Diez raised his hands in surrender. "Hey. I wasn't insinuating anything. It was just a thought I thought you should know. I was wrong and I'm going to shut up and go away now."

Zaid stretched his fingers having unknowingly balled his hands into fists. It seemed like, mating bond or not, he would have ended up going crazy for her.

Look at Diez. Not even a week and she'd already turned one of his best men against him. He suddenly wanted to reserve a room downstairs and line it with plastic.

He really was on edge. He wanted to kill Diez for trying to do the job he'd tasked him to do. His grandpa was right. This situation was crazy-inducing.

Everyone seemed to be bitching to him about not marrying Lauren when he was the one, more than anyone, who wanted her tied to him forever. If his closest friend, his grandfather, and his right-hand man were all telling him the same thing: stop fighting with her. Maybe he should listen. Annoyed, Zaid decided he and Lauren needed to talk.

CHAPTER VIII

Lauren

Lauren flopped face down onto the bed. She flapped her arms around and wiggled, sinking deeper into the duvet. This was the most comfortable bed she'd ever lain on. She wished she could take it with her when she escaped. Not that she had a plan. First she had to find a way to quietly drag Bonnie through the gates. That was going to be a whole ordeal considering how attached Bonnie was to Clyde. She was busy waving her arms over the sheets and casually planning an espionage—not even sure if she was using the word correctly—when Zaid suddenly walked in.

She jumped upright and watched him walk to the foot of the bed. "So you finally decide to show your face."

He looked around the room as if he didn't own it, like he was checking how much she'd rearranged the furniture. She hadn't. Well... except for her office corner. She'd surrounded herself with the little stuff toys she'd collected over the years. "How have you liked it here?"

She scowled at him. "As much as a prisoner can."

Zaid sighed. "You are *not* a prisoner." He shoved a hand through his hair and mumbled under his breath, "Why does everybody keep saying that?"

"Who else said it?" Lauren asked, curious and honestly, a little annoyed. She was treated well, and apart from Diez and Zaid, she hadn't complained to anybody. Who was sticking their nose in their business?

He was visibly upset, pacing around and putting his hands on his hips then removing them. It made her want to go comfort him, which made her even more annoyed. "You are not a prisoner. You have everything you could ever need or want. I'll give you anything and everything."

"Just don't leave right?" she asked to which he nodded reluctantly. "Zaid, what you're describing is a gilded cage."

He puffed out a frustrated breath. "How can I protect you if you're not here with me?"

"You already did," she said softly. "Gerald had taken a year of my life. I want to enjoy my life from now on."

He flinched. "And you're not enjoying it here. With me."

Lauren stayed quiet. How could she answer that when she was sitting on the best bed on the planet? She'd eaten the best apple pie she'd ever tasted as a snack. She'd had the best orgasms of her life in the basement below. Hell, even her dog was out there enjoying herself with her new boyfriend. Objectively speaking, just like he'd said before, she had everything she wanted and more. This was a better life if she was willing to overlook the circumstances that brought her here.

Zaid's shoulders dropped. "Little rabbit, I want nothing but your safety and happiness."

Lauren sighed. "I know. You've said that multiple times. I get it."

"But?"

"But I need my independence."

"I didn't steal it!"

"You did. You kidnapped me."

"I did it for you!"

Lauren's answer was a raised eyebrow. There was no point in talking if the other person wasn't going to listen.

"Fine! Will you be happy if you can go out for a walk? Or shop outside?"

"Yes, I'll be happy to get out and walk."

"Diez will escort you."

One step at a time. "Okay."

CHAPTER IX

Lauren

Lauren had insisted that they go to the park near her old apartment. Of course, Zaid protested. But she'd argued that the whole point of this little outing was so she could regain something from her old routine. Zaid had given in with a deep sigh.

"I'm assigning additional security personnel."

"Cool. But we're leaving. Now. I want to catch the sunset. They can catch up," she replied breezily.

Zaid gripped her chin and lifted it up so he could glare at her properly. "You're being a brat."

She replied with a saccharine smile. Somehow that worked. He let her go and nodded to Diez.

In the car Diez winked at her through the rearview mirror. "You shouldn't push him too much." Lauren rolled her eyes. "But. I have to say you're doing well."

She shifted her head away, refusing to acknowledge him, hiding the satisfied smile playing on her lips.

* * *

Lauren had forgotten how refreshing walking outside was. The air was fresher but it was also a little too cold and dry. The pavement was firm under her feet. It kind of hurt. She was wearing a little too much clothes. And there were people everywhere.

But this was great! Surely, after a few minutes of walking, she would start to feel better. She didn't bother to glance or check in with Diez. She just grabbed Bonnie's leash and opened the door.

They made it a few feet when Bonnie started fighting the leash.

"What is it? Let's go walk!" Lauren looked around. There was no one. She looked down at Bonnie who just barked again. They stood there, staring at each other.

"What's wrong?" Diez asked, catching up to them.

"She won't move. She's usually excited for walks."

"She probably misses Clyde."

Lauren groaned in frustration. Diez had a point. Her dog probably missed her boyfriend. And the house. And the expensive treats they give her. Lauren could hardly blame the pittie. She'd grown to love the spacious workspace and the coffee machine in that house.

But she was determined to make the most out of today. She'd fought for her walk and she was going to enjoy it goddamnit!

Lauren marched her way to their usual route, pulling on the leash, ignoring the uneasy feeling in her gut that had been plaguing her since they'd arrived at the park.

It was just nerves. Gerald was dead. She was safe. Diez was right there. Bonnie was right here. If only that stupid voice in her head stopped telling her she was being brat, she'd be fine. The sun was setting in a few minutes. She'd take pictures go back home.

She heard a grunt behind her followed by Bonnie's snarl. Lauren jerked back, but before she could see what had made Bonnie react that way, a wet fabric closed over her mouth and an unfamiliar toxic smell filled her nostrils. Cold dread formed at the pit of her stomach just at the same time as she lost consciousness.

Her head was pounding as hard as her panicked heart. It felt like every vein in her body throbbed with alarm. Add to that, this place smelled stale, like someone hadn't opened the windows in a week. *Everything* about this situation was unpleasant. She tried to move but her hands were tied up. She slowly opened her eyes. The carpet was oddly familiar. Two feet clad in beat-up leather shoes stepped into her vision.

She was not alone.

"What did you do to my brother?" The voice was raspy and unfamiliar.

So *this* was what a real kidnapping felt like. She suddenly felt bad for arguing with Zaid about her situation.

Lauren finally looked up, and his slitted eyes slammed against hers. On second thought, he looked a little familiar. Lauren's eyes darted around, finally taking in her full surroundings. That cabinet at the corner with its dinged-up wooden handle was hers. That scratched-up door knob with its tarnished belonged to her front door. She was in her old living room.

He'd brought her to her *old apartment*! This space was proving to be a solidly *not fun* place for her.

"Answer me!"

Lauren flinched. *Not the time to be daydreaming.* "Brother?" she croaked out through a sore throat.

"Gerald," the stranger growled.

Oh. Now she could see the resemblance.

A shot of pure outrage coursed through her. Why the hell was this guy upset at her? Sure, Zaid sank his brother to the ground, but Gerald deserved it. She couldn't care less about Gerald who was probably in a ditch, under concrete, somewhere. He deserved every inch of dirt he was under. She'd defend Zaid's actions to death.

She lifted her chin. "I think the better question would be what he did to me."

"Gerald loved you!"

They could spend the whole night arguing and nobody would win. Besides what was the point? He had a gun to her head.

Zaid would be looking for her by now. Diez—where was Diez? Where was Bonnie? Her heart stuttered, but she refused to let the panic overwhelm her. Zaid would find her. She was sure of it.

She fervently hoped they were both okay.

"I'm going to kill you."

Lauren felt it was a redundant thing to say, what with him pointing a gun to her head. But she kept her mouth shut because she didn't doubt for a second he'd shoot her with it. She did, however, manage to cut off her ties using the blade she'd inserted into the gap under the cushion of her chair. Her lazy sewing job had paid off.

He shifted away from her. In a split-second decision, Lauren launched herself to where she kept her baseball bat. She swung at him and heard a satisfying *thwack.* She didn't check where she'd hit him. She raced to the door, heart pounding out of her chest.

She managed to open her front door when she was yanked back by her hair. This was it. She was done. She was in the process of accepting her fate when she heard familiar scratchy noises followed by an angry growl. Her eyes darted downwards. Bonnie! Her heart filled with joy then dread. Her beloved baby was alive and currently preparing to attack a man armed with a gun.

"Bonnie no!"

Her shout was too late. Bonnie leaped and bit the stranger in the arm.

Eyes filled with pure crazed hate, Gerald's brother tried to shake her dog off, but that only made Bonnie lodge her fangs deeper into his limb. He let her go to try and push Bonnie off.

Lauren seized the opportunity, landing a powerful blow that sent Gerald's brother staggering backward. Bonnie let go. Lauren grabbed the gun and pointed it at him.

Teeth bared, Bonnie stood by her side, still growling at the stranger.

Gerald's brother pulled out a concealed knife and sneered at them. "I'm going to carve your dog up nicely."

No. There was no hesitation. Lauren pulled the trigger. Her aim was off, she targeted his chest, but the bullet blew off a part of his mouth.

Time stopped for a moment. He stared at her in shock, mouth literally gaping open. Maybe he wasn't dead after all?

Bonnie leapt and clamped her jaw on his throat.

The stranger finally fell. Blood spurted out of his neck. Bonnie still didn't let go.

It was over.

She still held the gun in the same position. Her legs wouldn't move. She looked up as a shadow of a man filled her open door. It wasn't over! She whirled around, trying to fix the gun on the new target—it was Zaid.

It was Zaid.

"Zaid!" she cried out, gun finally dropping to her side. That was when she realize tears were running down her face.

CHAPTER X

Zaid

She was here. She was alive. Zaid tried to comfort himself by repeating the truth over and over in his head.

He'd heard the gunshot from outside and he almost died. It was the most excruciating pain. He thought she was hurt, that he'd lost her. It turned out she'd just killed someone.

Zaid remembered how his first kill felt. He'd thrown up the entire contents of his stomach that night, and he was built for this. He'd been born into this world. Lauren wasn't. She shouldn't have needed to pull the trigger or even hold a gun. Violence was his job. He was supposed to protect her. He had failed her.

But looking into her wide eyes, he put aside his feelings of inadequacy and opened his arms. She stepped into them immediately. Today wasn't about him. He could beat himself up while he held her. His brave girl needed him to be steady right now.

Zaid slowly unhooked the gun from her fingers. "It's okay, love, I saw him. You did good. Such a good girl." Once he had the gun safety back in place, he cradled her to him, savoring her warmth and the strong beat of her heat. "Please do not scare me like that ever again."

She hiccuped. "Where's Diez?"

"Hospital."

"Is he–?"

"He's fine. Mostly he's worried about you and angry at himself." He didn't like Lauren worrying about another guy. But most of all, he hated the watery quality of her voice. He pulled her closer, needing to give her comfort, trying to convince himself she was fine. She was right here, safe, in his arms, and he was never going to let her go ever again. Except she was probably going to hate him if he did.

He realized he was the one trembling. His brave girl might be fighting back tears but she felt steady and strong against him.

"I promised to take care of you." Even to his ears, his voice sounded rough. "I don't think I am capable of letting you go anywhere ever again. Please don't ask that from me, little rabbit."

"I'm not. I won't. I don't want you to leave." She snuggled deeper into him. "I'm sorry. You're not a bad guy. You've helped me with Gerald and *this*."

"No, little rabbit," he couldn't help but butt in. "I might have taken care of Gerald, but I'm replacing him with a more obsessive, more dangerous man. Me."

"*No.* This might not make sense to other people, and I keep fighting it, but I realized it doesn't have to make sense to anyone else but us. We're–I don't know how else to put it. We're meant to be."

His heart expanded in his chest. It was scary and wonderful at the same time. This beating living organ in his chest couldn't possibly handle this much emotion. "Are you sure little rabbit? Once we're together, that's it."

"Yes, I'm sure. I think..." She lifted her chin. "I think I am already in love with you."

Zaid scoffed. "I've loved you the moment I laid eyes on you." He dropped a kiss on her hair. "I'm not sure if you still need time to digest this but it's best if you get used to it now. Me and you love, we're it. Forever. Accept it."

Lauren shook her head as if in bemusement before grinning up at him. "I'm done overthinking what I should or shouldn't be doing. Take me home, Zaid."

Zaid's phone beeped. He would've ignored it, except this was Dom's ringtone.

"I'm sorry, little rabbit. I need to take this." He hated how easily she let him go. Pissed off, he answered the call.

"The target is in front of my fucking building." Dom's voice was quiet. Scary quiet. That meant he was very *very* angry.

"Brave rat." Dom was talking about the rat that had been dirtying their city. The one they'd been hunting down for months. Looks like they'd underestimated how stupid the target was. As much as Zaid wanted to unleash all his pent-up frustration on the rat—"I'm with Lauren." His priorities had shifted. Lauren needed him.

"She okay?"

"She needs me." Or he needed to be with her. Semantics.

"I'll take care of this. It'd been a long time since I've made an example of someone anyway." Dom ended the call. The rat was getting the shorter end of the stick. While Zaid was efficient in their line of work, Dom was more thorough.

Dom must be furious. He'd kept that building pretty clean since Sophie came in. Oh well, it was about time he showed his true colors to her anyway. That was the only way they were going to be able to move forward.

For now, Zaid needed to bring his little rabbit home.

Epilogue

Zaid

Something was wrong. The tension was so thick in The Miranda Tower that Zaid had a hand on his gun while waiting for whatever it was to drop. Sophie stared at her laptop like a snow sculpture. No wave. No smile. If this was what's going on the whole day, Dom must be losing his mind. Zaid could relate, recalling the week when he tried to keep his distance from Lauren.

"Everything okay?"

"Yup."

He glanced at Sophie. "Uhh... pest control went fine?"

A muscle ticked in Dom's jaw. "I took care of it."

"You fired our cleaning crew."

"They took too long to do the job," Dom growled.

There was a screech in the air as Sophie's chair dragged over the floor. "Excuse me." She almost ran out of the room.

"What the hell is going on?" Zaid demanded to Dom once the door closed. "Did you piss her off? Did *I* piss her off?"

Dom turned away, looking out the window like a quintessential tortured mafia boss. Zaid almost laughed but then he said, "She was here when the rat came."

"Well, shit." What was there to say about that? Dom was obsessed with keeping their illegal business away from this place ever since Sophie came. But then again, Zaid very much doubted Sophie didn't already know something. "You need to talk to her."

Dom didn't say anything.

"Do you want me to talk to her?"

Dom whirled, and Zaid knew he was seconds and inches away from being punched. "The hell you will!"

Zaid raised his hands. He knew better than to poke a bad tempered lion. Dom was operating like one of the Cervantes men while they were in the middle of chasing after their woman.

"I'll handle it."

"Okay." Zaid shrugged. "You do that. For the meantime, I'm going home to my wife." He couldn't help the smug smile that graced his lips. That same smile stayed on his face and only widened when he opened the door to Lauren's office in their home.

She was sitting in her ergonomic chair with Bonnie, Clyde, and their litter of three puppies sleeping at her feet. She waved at him and he sat his ass on the armchair she'd placed beside her table. It was a nice comfortable leather chair that he liked to think she reserved for him. After all, nobody else visited *his wife* at *their home*. Yes, those words would never ever get old. She finished her work session with a couple more strokes and lines then she gave him her full attention.

"Welcome home. You seem like you're in a good mood."

He'd been in the best moods ever since they got married. He was obsessed and while he was unapologetic, he was trying this new thing called 'restraint'. "I love you," he decided to say instead.

Her face broke into a smile so bright he almost fell down to his knees to worship the sun that was *his wife*.

"Are you ready to take a break?"

"Uh huh. Ready for you." She slowly slipped out of her chair, sinking down to the floor.

Christ. He loved his wife. Everyday was beloved because of her. He leaned back and pushed his hips out, ready to be burnt alive by her heat.

Other Books

Read about Dom and Sophie's first in the ***hot and steamy*** short story:
Snowed In

In the mood for a romantic comedy with a touch of angst?
Falling for the Scrooge Next Door

Falling for the Girl Boss

Falling for the Heiress

More shorts? Unscripted Series: Three second-chance romance quick reads. There will be steamy scenes and some swearing.
Unraveling Unscripted Secrets
Rekindling Unscripted Love
Producing Unscripted Affairs

Sign up to my newsletter to stay updated:
http://eepurl.com/hWjT3b

Visit my website:
https://authormarimendoza.wordpress.com/

Printed in Dunstable, United Kingdom